"I saw Jesus," said Mary.
"Did not," said Thomas. "Jesus died."

"We saw Jesus, too," said the men.
"Did not," said Thomas.

"Did too!" said the men.
"I did not see Jesus," said Thomas.

"Let me see Jesus,"
said Thomas.

"We see Jesus," said the men.

"See me," said Jesus.

"You died. You left forever!"
said Thomas.

"Did not!" said Jesus.

Mary sat by Jesus.
Martha got fish.

Mary sat by Jesus.
Martha got salt.

Mary sat by Jesus.
Martha got a pan.

Mary sat by Jesus.
Martha got milk.

Mary sat by Jesus.
Martha got mad.

"Get Mary to help,"
Martha said to Jesus.

"No," said Jesus.
"Martha, sit still."

Mary sat by Jesus.
Martha sat by Jesus.
No one got mad.

Mary cried.
"He is dead," she said.

They cried.
"He is dead," they said.

Jesus cried.
"Roll the rock," he said.

"Come out,"
Jesus said.

"He is not dead!"
Mary said.

"He is alive!"
they said.

They were glad.

"He is alive!"
they said.

Jesus had dirty feet.

No one gave him
water for his feet.

No one gave him
oil for his feet.

No one gave him
a kiss.

Mary came.

She gave him sweet oil.

She gave him a kiss.

Jesus had sweet feet.

"Give me gold,"
said the man.

"Give me gold,"
he said.

"No," said Peter.
"We have no gold."

"But we have God,"
said Peter.

"Get up!"
said Peter.

"I am up!"
said the man.

"Give me God!"
said the man.

"He is up?" she said.
"Give *me* God!"